WELCOME TO
PASSPORT TO READING
A beginning reader's ticket to a brand-new world!

Every book in this program is designed to build read-along and read-alone skills, level by level, through engaging and enriching stories. As the reader turns each page, he or she will become more confident with new vocabulary, sight words, and comprehension.

These PASSPORT TO READING levels will help you choose the perfect book for every reader.

READING TOGETHER
Read short words in simple sentence structures together to begin a reader's journey.

READING OUT LOUD
Encourage developing readers to sound out words in more complex stories with simple vocabulary.

READING INDEPENDENTLY
Newly independent readers gain confidence reading more complex sentences with higher word counts.

READY TO READ MORE
Readers prepare for chapter books with fewer illustrations and longer paragraphs.

This book features sight words from the educator-supported Dolch Sight Words List. This encourages the reader to recognize commonly used vocabulary words, increasing reading speed and fluency.

For more information, please visit passporttoreadingbooks.com.

Enjoy the journey!

Little, Brown and Company

Hachette Book Group
1290 Avenue of the Americas, New York, NY 10104
Visit us at lb-kids.com

Little, Brown and Company is a division of Hachette Book Group, Inc.
The Little, Brown name and logo are trademarks of Hachette Book Group, Inc.

The publisher is not responsible for websites (or their content)
that are not owned by the publisher.

First Edition: April 2015

Library of Congress Control Number: 2014956323

ISBN 978-0-316-25641-4

10 9 8 7 6 5 4 3

CW

PRINTED IN THE UNITED STATES OF AMERICA

Passport to Reading titles are leveled by independent reviewers applying the standards developed by Irene Fountas and Gay Su Pinnell in *Matching Books to Readers: Using Leveled Books in Guided Reading*, Heinemann, 1999.

MARVEL

AVENGERS

AGE OF ULTRON

Friends and Foes

By **Tomas Palacios**

Illustrated by **Ron Lim**, **Andy Smith**, and **Andy Troy**

Based on the Screenplay by **Joss Whedon**

Produced by **Kevin Feige**, p.g.a.

Directed by **Joss Whedon**

LB

LITTLE, BROWN AND COMPANY
New York   Boston

Attention, Avengers fans!
Look for these words
when you read this book.
Can you spot them all?

scepter

robot

shield

arrow

A magical scepter is hidden inside a fortress.
It can be used for evil.

The Avengers must get the scepter.
They do not want it to fall into
the wrong hands.
They want to protect it from villains.

Tony Stark is Iron Man.

Iron Man's suit is very strong.

He can fly and fire missiles.

Iron Man's team of robots is called
the Iron Legion.
Sometimes the Avengers call the
Iron Legion for help!

Steve Rogers is Captain America.

His red, white, and blue shield

is indestructible.

Cap fights for the Avengers to get the scepter.

The Incredible Hulk is the strongest Avenger.

He is not always big and green.

When he is calm,

he is scientist Bruce Banner.

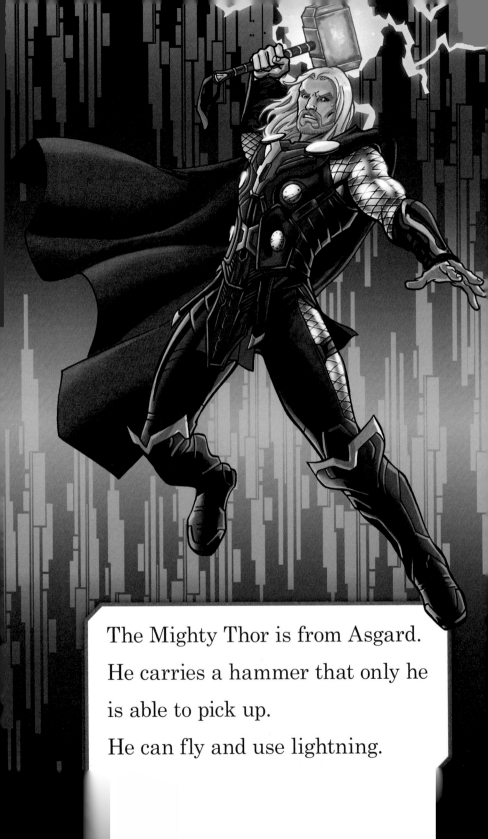

The Mighty Thor is from Asgard.

He carries a hammer that only he is able to pick up.

He can fly and use lightning.

Hawkeye never misses a shot.
He uses his bow and special arrows
to stop enemies.

Black Widow is a super-spy who fights hard.
She has weapons on her wrists
called Widow's Bites.
They zap enemies.

Now the Avengers have
the scepter.
They board the Quinjet and fly
back to Avengers Tower.
The Quinjet is very fast.

The Avengers study the scepter.

They learn how much power it possesses

and what it is capable of doing.

The Avengers must protect it from all threat

One threat is Ultron.

He wants the scepter from the Avengers.

He wants to take over the world.

Ultron has help from Wanda and her twin brother.

Wanda can attack minds.

The Avengers cannot get close to her.

She makes them think of nightmares.

Pietro is Wanda's brother.

He is so fast that no Avengers can catch him.

Together the twins try to help Ultron get the scepter from the Avengers.

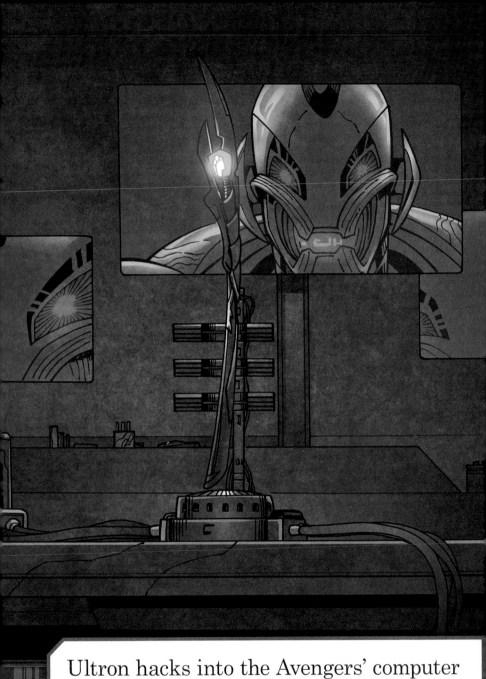

Ultron hacks into the Avengers' computer system and studies the scepter.

Now he has a plan!

Ultron takes over the Iron Legion.

They must now obey Ultron.

The robots burst through the window
and attack the Avengers!

The Iron Legion fire laser beams from their palms.
The Avengers fight back!

Hulk smashes and Black Widow punches.
Captain America uses his shield
to take out the robots.

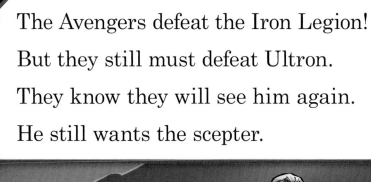

The Avengers defeat the Iron Legion!

But they still must defeat Ultron.

They know they will see him again.

He still wants the scepter.

Ultron is now ready to battle the Avengers face-to-face!

The Avengers find Ultron in South Africa.
He is with an army of Sentries.

The Avengers jump into battle!
But there are too many Sentries!
The Avengers cannot keep up.
The Hulk roars!

Black Widow and Thor attack
the Sentries and even Ultron himself!

Iron Man lands a blow against Ultron!
It seems to be working!
The Sentries are getting weak!
Time for the team to come together
and finish them off!

The Avengers assemble!
Hawkeye fires a trick arrow
and a Sentry explodes!

Thor unleashes lightning.

Iron Man fires his repulsor beams.

Cap throws his shield.

Whoosh!

The Avengers stopped Ultron,
but the evil robot will return.
The Avengers will assemble
and save the day once again!